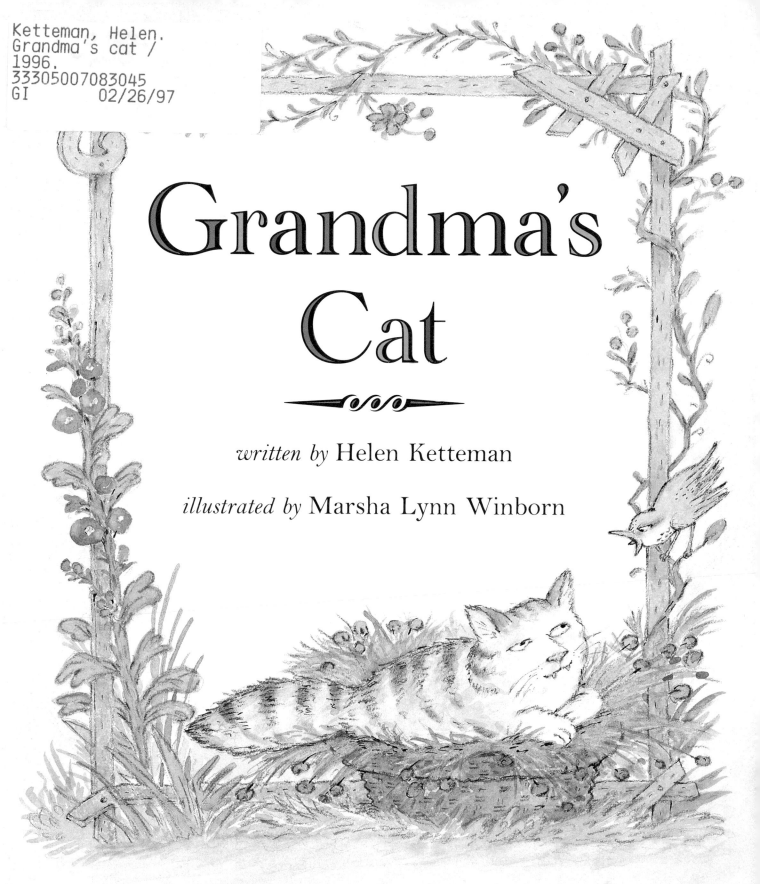

Grandma's Cat

written by Helen Ketteman

illustrated by Marsha Lynn Winborn

HOUGHTON MIFFLIN COMPANY / Boston 1996

For information about this and other Houghton Mifflin
trade and reference books and multimedia products, visit
The Bookstore at Houghton Mifflin on the World Wide Web
at http://www.hmco.com/trade/.

Manufactured in the United States of America

Book design by David Saylor
The text of this book is set in 26-point Monotype Bell.
The illustrations are watercolor with colored ink
and pencils, reproduced in full color.

WOZ   10 9 8 7 6 5 4 3 2 1

Library of Congress Cataloging-in-Publication Data
Ketteman, Helen.
Grandma's cat / by Helen Ketteman ;
illustrated by Marsha Lynn Winborn p.   cm.
Summary: An eager child finds that it takes time and
patience to make friends with Grandma's cat.
ISBN: 0-395-73094-5
[1. Cats—Fiction. 2. Stories in rhyme.]
I. Winborn, Marsha, ill.   II. Title.
PZ8.3.K46Gr   1996   [E]—dc 20
95-3281   CIP   AC

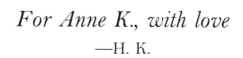

For Anne K., with love
—H. K.

For our mom—not a grandma,
but a Grand Ma
—M. L. W.

Grandma's cat
is round and fat.

He hides.
I seek.

He scoots.
I peek.

He climbs a tree.

I scrape my knee.

He's up the stair.
I chase him there.

I pounce, but miss.

He gives a hiss.

He's on the rail.

I grab his tail.

He claws my nose.

I yowl.

He goes.

He's near the gate.
I stop, then wait.

I stoop down low.

He starts to go.

I speak. He hears.
He turns his ears.

Kitty Kitty Kitty Kitty

I bring a treat
he likes to eat.

He tastes.

He stays.

I stroke.

He plays.

I sit. I clap.

He tries my lap.

His tail has burrs.
I pick. He purrs.

That night in bed
I scratch his head.

He purrs again.

I've made a friend.